Little Animals Lost

by Ana Galan
Illustrated by Pablo Pino

To Michael, so he doesn't stray away.
—A.G.

For my little Agostina,
because she brings me back to earth when I'm lost.
—P.P.

ISBN 978-0-545-49835-7

Text copyright © 2013 by Ana Galan.
Illustrations copyright © 2013 by Pablo Pino.

12 11 10 9 8 7 6 5 4 3 2   17 18/0

Printed in the U.S.A.   40
First printing, April 2013

Little Animals Lost

by Ana Galan
Illustrated by Pablo Pino

Scholastic Inc.

Eight good friends go out to play.
They run and jump and leap all day!

They look around.
They went too far!
And now they don't
know where they are.

"Baa baa baa," cries shy Lamb.
"Where's our home with Farmer Sam?
I don't know where I am!"

"Meow meow meow," says Kitty.
"These big trees are not so pretty.
We are lost! Oh, what a pity!"

Duckling says, "Quack quack quack.
What if those bees begin to attack?

What if it rains, the sky turns black?
What if we can't find our way back?!"

Small Calf cries, "Moo moo moo,
I'm hungry . . . and thirsty, too!

Mommy, Mommy, where are you?"

"Oink oink oink," Piglet cheers.
"We will find her. No more tears.
 It's not as bad as it appears."

"Neigh neigh neigh," brave Colt replies.
"Look around. Open your eyes. See
this meadow? And the blue skies?"

"Woof woof woof!" Puppy calls. "I see horses! I see stalls! There's your mom! I hear her calls!"

"Peep peep peep," says soft Chick.
"Yes, there she is! Let's go there, quick!"

"Baa baa! Meow! Oink oink! Moo!
We looked all over for you!"

"Cluck cluck! Woof! Neigh neigh! Quack!
We're so happy you are back!"

"Quack quack! Woof! Cluck cluck! Neigh! Safe and sound! Don't stray away."

"Oink oink! Baa! Meow meow! Moo!
Sweet dreams, babies. We love you!"

Parent to Parent: Staying Safe

Dear Parents,

Getting lost is a very upsetting experience, both for the child and the parents. No matter how careful you are, sometimes children get distracted and wander away. It happens to hundreds of families every year, and in the overwhelming majority of the time, it ends happily.

In my experience, there are a few simple things you can do to prepare your family for a situation like this:

- Make sure your child knows your complete name.

- Write your name, address, and phone number on a card and put it in your child's pocket, or make a little necklace with this information that she/he can wear. Depending on the age of your child, she/he can also memorize your phone number and address instead.

- Take a picture of your child with your cell phone before you leave your home. That way, if she/he wanders away, you'll have a recent picture on hand and can remember what she/he was wearing.

- When going to a crowded public location, establish a meeting place in the area in case you are separated. Make sure your child remembers that spot.

- Talk to her/him about what to do if she/he ever loses sight of you. Remind her/him that she/he shouldn't try to look for you on her/his own. Instead, she/he should find another mom with children to help.

- Stay calm. Think positive. And remember to ask for help.

Learning about safety is an important part of growing up. You can use this book to talk to your child about what she/he should do if she/he gets lost.

Before you start reading, look at the illustration on the cover with your child and read the title out loud. Ask her/him, "What do you think is going to happen in the story?" Give your child time to answer. Then start reading the story. As you read, point at the baby animals and ask your child if she/he knows their names and the sounds they make. You may want to point at the animal sounds in the text and let your child read along.

Once you finish the story, ask her/him questions like: "What did the animals do when they got lost?" "How did they find their way back home?" "What would you do if you got lost like the baby animals in the book?" Use this opportunity to talk with your child about staying safe.

Don't forget to reassure your child that if she/he ever gets lost, you will never stop looking for her/him until you find her/him.

Sincerely,
Ana